The AMAZING DAYS of ABBY HAYES

The Pen Is Mightier Than the Sword

ANNE MAZER

AN
APPLE
PAPERBACK

SCHOLASTIC INC.
New York Toronto London Auckland Sydney
Mexico City New Delhi Hong Kong Buenos Aires

For Kate, at the other end of the purple phone!

ISBN 0-439-17882-7

12 11 10 9 8 7 6 5   2 3 4 5 6/0

Printed in the U.S.A   40

First Scholastic printing, December 2001

Chapter 1

Thursday

"Do what you like."
— François Rabelais

School Rules Calendar

Last week our creative writing teacher, Ms. Bunder, announced that our fiflh-grade class will publish a school newspaper. We will  brainslorm ideas today. But I don't need to brainstorm. I already know what I'd like to do:

Cover important school events.
Get exclusive interviews.
Write stories that the entire school will talk about for months!

Be the star reporter!

Yes! I will do what I like! All of it! I
will! I will!

At the front of the fifth-grade classroom, Ms. Kantor and Ms. Bunder whispered to each other.

The fifth-graders were finishing a math quiz. Abby Hayes looked up from her paper and wondered if the two teachers were talking about the newspaper. Maybe Ms. Bunder was recommending her as the star reporter right now! Then she shook her head. She couldn't guess what they were talking about — and, anyway, she couldn't dream about the newspaper when she still had fractions to deal with.

Abby scratched out a mistake and began to recalculate. Next to her, her best friend, Jessica, had already finished the quiz and was doodling on her notebook cover. Natalie, her other close friend, was staring at the ceiling.

Ms. Bunder rummaged through a pile of papers on the desk while Ms. Kantor picked up a small bell. A restless murmur went through the room.

"Two minutes!" Ms. Kantor announced, ringing

the bell. "If you're finished early, sit quietly at your desks. That means you, Zach and Tyler!"

Ms. Kantor was their regular teacher; Ms. Bunder came in once a week. She was a young woman who barely looked older than Abby's fourteen-year-old twin sisters. Only a few years ago, Ms. Bunder baby-sat Ms. Kantor's kids. Now she taught creative writing to Ms. Kantor's fifth-graders!

Abby rushed to finish the last few problems. As she began the second-to-last one, Ms. Kantor rang the bell again. "Time's up!"

With a sigh, Abby put down her pen. She had *almost* finished. That was good for her. Math was her worst subject. Creative writing was her best. All week long, she looked forward to Ms. Bunder's class.

She handed her paper to Ms. Kantor and went up to Ms. Bunder.

"Yes, Abby?" Ms. Bunder smiled. "What can I do for you today? Have you written a novel since last week? Or maybe you've composed a play?"

"I've only been writing in my journal, Ms. Bunder." Abby pushed a lock of curly red hair away from her face.

"That's wonderful!" her teacher encouraged her.

"But I want to do more," Abby continued. "I want to be a reporter for the class newspaper."

"You're a natural," Ms. Bunder agreed.

"Really?" Abby said. "The star reporter? Do you think I could?"

"Of course." Ms. Bunder picked up a folder lying on the table next to her. "You'd succeed at any writing assignment, Abby."

"*Yes!*" Abby glanced over at Natalie and Jessica and gave them a thumbs-up sign.

Ms. Bunder smiled at her again. "Just remember that we're picking assignments out of a hat," she warned. "It's all in the draw. Let's hope that today will be your lucky day."

Ms. Kantor clapped her hands for attention. "Creative writing is about to begin! Everyone get out your notebooks."

As Abby hurried back to her seat, Ms. Bunder went to the front of the room.

"What does a newpaper do?" she asked the class. "Does anyone know?"

Brianna's hand shot into the air. "I'm going to be a gossip columnist!" she announced. As usual, she looked as if she had stepped out of a teen fashion catalog. She wore a short, strappy dress and chunky shoes. Her lips gleamed from the colored lip gloss she wore. "I'll report on all the fifth-grade parties. I'll let everyone know who the most popular kids are. Like me."

"Yay, Brianna," her best friend, Bethany, chirped on cue.

Ms. Bunder shook her head. "A gossip column doesn't belong in a school newspaper, Brianna. But I'm glad you brought up the word 'columnist.' "

She picked up a piece of chalk and wrote on the board. " 'Columnist' is an important word for every newspaper. Who knows what it means?"

"Someone who writes a column," Zach replied. He and his best friend, Tyler, were the resident fifth-grade computer fanatics. *"Duh."*

"And a column is — ?" Ms. Bunder prompted.

"An article in the paper," Jessica said. She held up a sketch of a newspaper's front page. "Like this," she said, pointing to one of the columns she had drawn.

"What kind of an article?" their teacher asked.

"A story!" Mason blurted out.

"A report of something that happened, like an accident or a crime," Natalie said.

"An opinion," Abby added. "What people think."

"You're all correct." Ms. Bunder wrote their answers on the board. "A column is a regular feature by the same writer. A newspaper is full of information. Some of it is fact, some of it is opinion." She put down the chalk and dusted off her hands. "Why do we want to publish one in our school?"

"For fun!" Jessica cried.

"For fame," Brianna insisted.

"To use computers," Zach and Tyler said in unison.

"To tell other kids stuff, like, you know, what's like happening in school." Mason burped loudly.

"He's so eloquent," Abby whispered to Jessica.

"That's right, Mason. We want to communicate with others and inform them about events." Ms. Bunder smiled at the class. "We'll let them know what's happening and what we think about it."

"Ms. Kantor will teach us a desktop publishing program. We'll publish the newspaper every two weeks and distribute it to the entire school."

The class cheered.

"We'll learn new writing skills," Ms. Bunder continued. "We'll learn about interview techniques, note taking, how to research a subject, and lots more."

"When do we start?" Abby asked.

"Right now." Ms. Bunder turned to the board again. "Keeping all of this in mind, let's brainstorm what we want in our newspaper."

"Cartoons!" Mason yelled.

"Jokes," Jessica added. "And sports."

"Science?" Jonathan suggested. He was a quiet, serious boy who didn't talk much.

Rachel raised her hand. "Interviews."

"Recipes?" Tyler suggested. "My brother cuts them out of the newspaper."

"Current events!" Abby cried. "School projects!"

Ms. Bunder wrote everyone's suggestions on the board. "Very good. Any others?"

"What about an advice column, Ms. Bunder?" Brianna said. "Kids could write in for advice on their problems." She glanced quickly around the classroom. "Not me, of course."

"A police blotter?" Natalie asked hopefully. She loved to read mysteries and do chemistry experiments in her basement. "I want to be the crime reporter."

"We don't have a lot of crime at Lancaster Elementary," Jessica said. "Unless you want to write about who stole what base during games."

"Or who took the pencils from the kindergarten classroom," Abby added.

"We'll pass on that one, Natalie," Ms. Bunder said. "I like the advice column, though. That's original, Brianna."

Abby frowned. Why hadn't *she* thought of it?

Ms. Bunder took a hat from a shelf. "Okay, everyone, it's time for the lottery!"

The class cheered.

"Write your name on a piece of paper," Ms. Bunder said. "Then drop it into the hat when I come around to your desk."

Abby pulled out her favorite purple pen. "Abby ('Purple') Hayes," she wrote with a flourish. "Purple Hayes" was Ms. Bunder's nickname for her. She folded up the paper, closed her eyes, and wished as hard as she could.

"School projects reporter, school projects reporter," she muttered. This was the assignment that would make her a star. "I want to be the school projects reporter!" She took a deep breath. "Maybe the current events reporter! Or even the sports reporter!"

Chapter 2

Thursday	(again)

"O aching time! O moments
big as years!"

— *John Keats*

Swiss Watch Calendar

<u>News Flash! From Ms. Bunder's Fifth-
Grade Classroom</u>

by Abby Hayes, Star Reporter-to-Be

The moments <u>are</u> as big as years as Ms.
Kantor's fifth-graders wait for Ms. Bunder
to pull their assignments out of a hat. The
creative writing teacher, normally one of the
most friendly and sympathetic teachers in
Lancaster Elementary, is taking <u>forever!</u> She
hasn't even started the lottery!

First, she lists all the newspaper jobs. She
has to write each one on the board, which
takes a long time. Then she asks the class

if she forgot anything. Mason reminds her of three assignments she's overlooked. Then Ms. Bunder makes a speech about everyone doing his or her best. She says that the class will rotate jobs in two months "so that everyone gets a chance to experience more than one role."

A public service message from your reporter: Ms. Bunder, please stop explaining and pick the names out of the hat!!!

The fifth-graders have earned a page in the Hayes Book of World Records for Most Perfect Patience During Daunting Delays.

Time hurts! It aches, too. I feel like I'm getting the flu from suspense!

<u>More Late-Breaking News!</u>
by You-Know-Who
Ms. Bunder is finally shaking up the names in the hat! Hooray, Ms. Bunder! Hooray! The fifth-graders are clutching

their lucky keychains, crossing their fingers, and wishing on stars. (Or wishing for star assignments!) Suddenly, without warning, the creative writing teacher puts down the hat.

"I forgot," she says. "We have to name our paper. Let's do that first."

The whole class groans. It is a mighty roar of despair and frustration.

"Calm down," Ms. Bunder says. "It'll only take a few minutes."

"Sshhh!" Ms. Kantor says.

The two teachers don't understand the sad plight of the fifth-graders. No one wants to think of names now, but the brave class quickly rallies. Here is what they come up with:

Jessica: Got News?
Mason: Elementary News
Bethany: The Weekly Woof (am surprised our resident hamster lover doesn't suggest The Nibble and Squeak)
Rachel: The Lancaster Lark
Zach: Bunder Bytes
Brianna: Fifth-Grade Herald

A vote is taken. The winner is <u>The Lancaster Lark</u>! Hooray! Ms. Bunder is now going to draw names out of the hat! The class is abuzz with anticipation.

<u>Another You-Know-What by You-Know-Who</u>

We bring you an up-to-the-minute report on the results of <u>The Lancaster Lark</u> lottery!!!

Excitement fills the fifth-grade classroom. Ms. Bunder pulls the first name out of the hat. He or she will be the sports reporter. And it's Mason!

He whoops in delight. Ms. Kantor puts her finger to her lips in warning.

The science reporter is next. Bethany's name emerges. Bethany looks confused for a moment. She doesn't like science. Then her face brightens. "I'll write about animals!" she cries. (She is the fifth-grader most likely to become a veterinarian.)

The Lancaster Lark photographer is Natalie. She looks disappointed. "I wanted to
be the crime reporter," she whispers.

Her face brightens when Ms. Bunder sug-
gests that she develop the photographs herself.

"Chemicals," Natalie says happily. "I love
darkrooms."

More lucky draws follow. Jessica will
work on design and layout. She is thrilled.
"I did not want to be a reporter," she
whispers to Abby.

Rachel gets the joke column, Zach the
cartoons, and Jonathan is the school
projects reporter. Abby Hayes is a little
disappointed. She wanted to be the
school projects reporter. But there are still
plenty of plum assignments left.
(That's what Ms. Bunder
calls them. Why aren't there
pear, or peach, or blueberry
assignments?)

Ms. Bunder draws the slip for
people profile reporter. Whoever gets it will

conduct interviews with people around the school. Abby Hayes holds her breath. Ms. Bunder unfolds the paper. "Congratulations, Brianna!" she says.

Brianna must have been born under a lucky star. Or maybe her parents bought her one.

"I've already picked out a name for my column," Brianna says.
" 'The Brianna Chronicles.' "

"Yay, Brianna,"
Bethany chirps. "Yay,
'Brianna Chronicles'!"

Is Brianna going to interview herself? Over and over and <u>over</u>?

Abby Hayes sighs. Luckily, there are still plum assignments left.

<u>Interruption</u>. We interrupt this news flash for another news flash!

Your reporter is so busy writing about everyone else's plum assignments that she doesn't hear her own!

She only realizes she's missed it when her friends start congratulating her.

Natalie makes a thumbs-up sign. Bethany grins.

Ms. Bunder looks pleased. Ms. Kantor is applauding.

Is Abby Hayes the current events reporter? Did Abby Hayes get the plum assignment of her dreams? Or did she get a rotten pear?

"Jessica! What am I?" she whispers.

"The advice columnist," her best friend whispers back. "You're our new 'Dear Abby.'"

Chapter 3

Friday

"One gives nothing so freely as advice."

— Duc de la Rochefoucauld

Nuts and Bolts Calendar

Oh, yeah? <u>Really???</u> I only give advice when I have to!

<u>Six Reasons Why I Can't Write the Advice Column for the School Newspaper</u>

1. I'm only ten years old. (But so is everyone in the class.)

2. I don't have a lot of experience.

3. What am I supposed to say when kids tell me their problems?

4. It was Brianna's idea; why can't <u>she</u> do it?

5. I'd be a better interviewer than Brianna.

6. <u>I don't want to!!!!!</u>

Most of the kids like their assignments. Jonathan plans to write about school

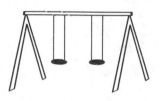 recycling practices. Rachel is collecting knock-knock jokes. Meghan is going to write about the new school playground equipment.

Bethany plans to do a scientific study of hamsters. Will she interview her hamster, Blondie? It might go like this:

Bethany: And how long have you lived in this cage?

Blondie: Squeak.

Bethany: Fascinating. You say your favorite activity is rolling on that wheel?

Blondie: Squeak.

Bethany: What kinds of food do you eat?

Blondie: Squeak.

Bethany: You're unusually intelligent, aren't you?

Blondie: Squeak.

Brianna has announced that she's devoting the "Brianna Chronicles" to the teachers of Lancaster Elementary.

"Teachers need our appreciation," she said with a gracious wave. "Otherwise they are unappreciated."

Ms. Kantor and Ms. Bunder smiled at her. They didn't notice that her sentence canceled itself out.

Bethany gets to interview her hamster, and Brianna gets to name her column after herself. Meghan and Jonathan get to write important articles. Only I am stuck solving other kids' problems!

It's no fair!!! Everyone is happy with the results of the lottery, except me.

<u>What My Friends and Teachers Said to Me</u>

"You can do it!" (Jessica)

"I'll take your picture." (Natalie)

"With your writing skills, you can handle anything." (Ms. Bunder)

"We have the right person for the job." (Ms. Kantor)

"Way to go, Abby!" (Zach)

I was <u>almost</u> beginning to feel okay about the advice column when Mason yelled out, "What are you going to call it?"

Before I could even think of an answer, he bellowed, "'Dear Abby'!"

I didn't mind it when Jessica said it. But then she didn't yell it out to the entire class.

When Mason did that, everyone laughed! (Except me.) For the rest of the day, my classmates called me "Dear Abby."

I'm not "Dear Abby." I don't know enough to give advice to <u>anyone</u>!

<u>Why</u> did I get stuck with this assignment???

Abby wrote the last few words with a flourish. She closed her journal and checked the clock. Time to get ready for school. She got up and glanced in the mirror.

As usual, her hair was a tangled, wild, curly red mess. No matter how often she brushed or smoothed it, it wouldn't behave. How was she supposed to solve others' problems when she couldn't even keep her hair in order?

She opened the drawer where she secretly kept her earrings.

"Dear Advice Columnist," she said out loud. "I am ten years old and my parents won't let me get my ears pierced."

What would the advice columnist say? Probably to make the best of a bad situation. It was the kind of advice that parents gave.

Abby slammed the drawer shut. She gazed for a moment at the calendars lining her walls. They were her daily inspiration. When Abby needed advice, she read her calendars. Could she consult them for her advice column, too?

Shaking her head, she grabbed her backpack and headed to Isabel's room to see T-Jeff before school.

T-Jeff was the kitten she and Isabel shared. His real name was Thomas Jefferson. Abby hadn't picked it out, of course.

"Dear Advice Columnist," she said again. "My sister Isabel, who loves history, insists on calling our kitten Thomas Jefferson. I can't argue because she is helping me take care of him."

Thomas Jefferson was too long a name for a little

gray kitten with blue eyes, Abby thought. She hoped he would grow into it.

She knocked on Isabel's door.

"Come in!" Isabel cried. She was sitting at her desk, reading a book. She wore a gold velvet skirt, a lace shirt, and long, dangling earrings. Her fingernails were newly painted blue and gold.

"I've just finished two weeks' homework in advance," Isabel said with satisfaction. "What's up?"

"I came to see T-Jeff," Abby said.

"He's under the bed." Isabel turned back to the book she was studying.

Abby crouched down to look. "Kitty, kitty!" she called. "T-Jeff!"

"Meow!" the kitten answered. He sprang at a dust ball. After wrestling with it for a moment, he scampered over to Abby.

"That's a dust ball, silly." Abby scratched him under his chin.

T-Jeff began to purr.

"Have you ever written an advice column?" Abby asked her older sister.

"No," Isabel replied. "Why?"

"I'm supposed to write one for my class newspaper."

"Easy. Just answer the questions people send you."

Isabel blew on her fingernails. "It's a no-brainer."

"What if they don't? What if no one needs advice?" Abby took a breath. "Even worse, what if I can't help?"

"Of course you can!" Isabel said. "Why not?" She checked her nails again and closed her book. "And everyone always needs advice! You're asking me advice right now."

Abby picked up T-Jeff and carried him over to the bed. "That's the problem. How can I *give* advice when I *need* it?"

"You're wiser than you think," Isabel said.

"That's easy for you to say." Abby frowned at her older sister. "You always have the answer to everything."

"Not true."

"I don't believe you." Abby made a mental list of her SuperSib's accomplishments. She was president of her class, a high honor student, and a champion debater. She acted in plays, knew all about history, and loved to do research on the Internet. She was also the world's reigning expert on manicures.

Isabel glanced at the clock. "It's getting late. Let's get breakfast. We shouldn't go to school on an empty stomach."

"See? You always know what to do." Abby petted T-Jeff one last time, then set him down on the floor.

"Don't worry so much, Abby. Have more confidence in yourself. You'll be fine!"

"You did it again," Abby pointed out.

Isabel rolled her eyes.

Abby followed her older sister down the stairs. "You can't help it, Isabel," she persisted. "You're a natural advice-giver. Like some people are natural soccer players or actors or math geniuses."

"And I thought I was just bossy," her older sister joked.

"Yes!" Isabel's twin, Eva, yelled from the top of the stairs. "You *are*!"

"Takes one to know one!" Isabel shot back. Like opposite charges, she and Eva often set off explosions.

"Isabel!" Abby cried out suddenly. The solution to all her problems was right here in front of her nose. Why hadn't she seen it before?

Her sister turned away from her twin. "What is it, Abby?"

"You can write the advice column for me!"

Chapter 4

<u>What Happened Yesterday After I Asked Isabel to Write My Column for Me</u>

Isabel laughed hysterically for about ten minutes, then wiped her eyes and said, "Forget it."

"Why won't you help me?" I demanded.

"Come on, Abby," Isabel urged. "You're a writing whiz! Didn't you rewrite the school play? Haven't you published an article in a real newspaper? Why do you want me to do your creative writing homework? You'd do it better.

"And anyway," she concluded, "'Dear Abby' sounds a lot better than 'Dear Isabel.'"

I scowled at her.

"You can do it," my older sister advised me. "You have nothing to fear but fear itself.'"

Wrong! I have lots of things to fear — for example, hearing Dear Abby jokes for the rest of my life. If the jokes keep up, I will change my name. Or start calling myself Abigail.

Nooooo! Anything but Abigail!

"I won't do it!" I said.

Isabel shook her head. "How can you disappoint your favorite teacher?"

She's right again. I can't disappoint Ms. Bunder. Ms. Bunder thinks I can do a good job. I have to write the column.

Resolutions

Make the best of the assignment.

Don't complain. (At least not too much.)

Think of a name for the column. (_NOT_
"Dear Abby.")

Names for My Column
Abby's Advice
Gabby Abby
The Abigail Hayes Advice Column
Hayes Helpline
Happy Helper
Dear A. H.
Hey, You!
Advice Column
To Whom It May Concern
Abby's Admonitions (this word means
"warnings")

News Flash! From Your Secret Star Reporter, Abby Hayes

The Secret Star Reporter is discouraged.
She wants to make the best of her assignment, but she can't do anything until the
questions start pouring in. For once in her
life, she wishes she were Brianna.

Yesterday Brianna set up interviews with
the principal, Ms. Yang, the gym teacher,

Mr. Stevens, and the creative writing teacher, Ms. Bunder.

Brianna has decided not to use "The Brianna Chronicles" for the title of her column. She is now calling it "Conversations with Brianna."

Will Brianna serve tea and homemade cookies during her "conversations"?

Will she have a film crew taping them?

Will she sell transcripts of her interviews for five dollars, plus shipping and handling?

The Secret Star Reporter is turning into the Storming Star Reporter. Abby Hayes needs some calming advice. She will go find her father. He always helps her when she has a problem.

Later: Dad was on the phone. I heard him say something about assisted living.

(My brother assists me with math homework. I assist with the dishes. I tried to get Isabel to assist me in advice-giving!

Don't we all get assistance in living? What is Dad talking about???)

Dad didn't explain assisted living. He was frowning. He waved me away.

"What's the matter, Dad?" I asked.

He looked like he needed help more than I did. Maybe this was my chance to give real, live advice.

"Can't you see I'm busy?" he said irritably.

I tiptoed out of his office. Dad is not often cranky. I hope he's okay. I wish he had let me give him advice. How will I know how to do it if I don't start practicing now?

Chapter 5

Saturday still

"Do cats eat bats? Do bats eat cats?"

— Lewis Carroll

Attic Calendar

Is Abby gabby? Or is Abby blabby? Is Gabby Abby a good name for my blabby advice column? Or should I be Dear A. H.? Is this a good question for my advice column?

Abby petted T-Jeff. Her kitten was curled up on a chair in her room.

"You don't need advice, and you don't give it, either," Abby said to him, petting him behind the ears. "You're perfect the way you are."

T-Jeff purred in response.

Abby plopped herself down on the bed. She lay

back and stared at the ceiling. For the first time, she noticed that it was the only place in her room where there weren't any calendars. It looked strangely empty.

Abby jumped up and walked around her room, studying the walls.

The Lightbulb Calendar and the Starry Night Calendar: Those two would be just right. She took them off the wall. Now, how was she going to get them up on the ceiling? She'd need a ladder, a hammer, nails, tape. . . .

Downstairs, the doorbell rang.

"Abby!" her little brother, Alex, called. "It's for you!"

"I'll be right there!" Shutting the door behind her so T-Jeff wouldn't escape from her room, Abby went downstairs.

Natalie and Bethany were in the hallway. Natalie had her camera slung over her shoulder. Bethany clutched a notebook with pictures of hamsters on its cover.

"Guess what we're doing?" Bethany chirped.

"I'm taking pictures of the new school playground for the newspaper," Natalie frowned. "I hope I find a crime to report, even though that's not my job."

"I'm collecting hamster stories for the science column," Bethany said. When she wasn't trailing Brianna, Bethany was a different person. She was friendly and fun to be around. "Want to come with us?"

"Well . . ." Abby hesitated. "I'm hanging calendars. I was just going to find a ladder."

"Find it later," Natalie urged. "Come with us instead."

"You're working on your newspaper assignments," Abby said. "What about me? I can't go door-to-door collecting problems!"

"If Bethany or I run into trouble, you'll help us," Natalie said. "You'll be our on-the-spot advice columnist."

Abby shook her head.

"You have one of the best assignments, Abby," Bethany said.

"Me? Are you serious? Why?"

"It was Brianna's idea, and Brianna always has great ideas," Bethany explained.

"Oh," Abby said. She wished Bethany had come up with a more convincing reason.

"It's true!" Natalie exclaimed. "How often do people listen to ten-year-olds? When you're an advice columnist, they want to hear your opinion. You get to tell them what to do."

Bethany added, "Everyone looks up to you."

"You'll find out their secret thoughts!" Natalie lowered her voice. "Maybe someone will confess a crime."

"I'll turn it over to you to investigate," Abby promised. She picked up her journal and tucked it into her coat pocket.

She had never thought of the advice column like that. Maybe it really was okay. Maybe it was even better than okay.

Half an hour later, Abby and Natalie stood together outside the school playground.

"Where do you think I should take this shot?" Natalie asked. She sighed. "I wish I was in the darkroom already."

"Over there," Abby said, pointing to the fence surrounding Lancaster Elementary.

Natalie dropped to her stomach and crawled through a gap in the bushes, emerging near the chain-link fence. She focused her camera and clicked the shutter. "Got it," she cried.

Natalie had already used up a roll of film. On Abby's advice, she had taken pictures lying down on the ground, from high in a tree, and from inside a jungle gym.

"I wonder how Bethany is doing," Natalie said as she emerged from the bushes. Her face had a scratch on it, and her hands were dirty.

"She's in hamster heaven," Abby said. "Last I saw her, she was getting stories from a group of third-graders."

Natalie pushed the rewind button on her camera. "That's roll number two," she said. "Good thing I brought lots of film."

"I can't wait to see how your pictures turn out!" Abby said.

Natalie made a face. "What if they're unfocused? Or poorly composed? Or just plain bad?"

"They'll be great!"

"That's easy for you to say," Natalie began.

"Abby! Natalie!" Bethany cried. She ran toward her friends, waving sheets of paper in the air. Her face glowed. "Guess what? I got eight different stories! All about hamsters!"

"Amazing," Natalie said.

"Is that enough for my column?" Bethany asked. "Do I need more? Or fewer?"

Abby thought for a moment. "I'd take the best three or four. People will get bored with too many hamster stories."

"They will?" Bethany said.

"Take Abby's advice," Natalie told her. "She knows all about writing."

"Advice?" Abby repeated slowly. "Did you say *advice*?"

Natalie nodded.

"Excuse me," Abby said to her friends. "I have something important to do." She sat down on a bench and pulled out her journal.

I just gave advice. <u>HOORAY!!!</u>
It was easy. Bethany liked it. So did Natalie.

I also gave advice to
Natalie about where to
shoot her pictures.

Do you know what this means?
It means I can do it. I <u>can</u> do it. I will

have fun doing it! (Repeat one hundred times each day, before breakfast, lunch, and dinner.)

But what if people ask for advice on serious problems? What will I do then? (Waaaaaaa! Mommmy!)

When I write to Grandma Emma, I ask her advice all the time. When she writes back, she always knows the right thing to say.

Resolution

When answering serious problems, imagine self as wise, kind, loving grandmother.

(Can I imagine myself with white, curly hair? Collecting salt-and-pepper shakers? Um, maybe not.)

No, will be talkative ten-year-old who loves to write, instead.

Another Resolution

I must prepare myself for this very important role!

Still More Resolutions

Read advice columns daily for inspiration.

Check out self-help books from library.

Absorb wisdom of ages. (Question: Which ages? I hope ten-year-olds are included.)

Brush up on letter-writing skills. Write to Grandma Emma more often.

I can do it. I can do it. I can do it.

My assignment is a ripe, juicy, delicious, tree-ripened plum. Yum!

I will be Gabby Abby.

Gabby Abby will give Brianna advice on how to do interviews. Gabby Abby will tell Bethany to stop saying "Yay, Brianna," all the time. She'll tell Ms. Yang how to run the school. She'll—

INTERRUPTION!

Natalie and Bethany are going to Bethany's house to take photos of Bethany and her hamster, Blondie. I'm going home. My friends got pictures and stories for their Lancaster Lark assignments. What did I get?

Abby's Advice Column Accomplishments

1. Found name.
2. Lost fear.
3. Gained excitement.

I can do it. I can do it. I can do it. I will have fun doing it. HOORAY!!!!!!

Chapter 6

Isabel said this to me last week! Is Ralph Waldo Emerson copying her?

I don't think so. The calendar says he lived more than a hundred years ago. If he went to school today, everyone would make fun of his name. Then he'd have to write to Gabby Abby for advice!

Yesterday I got up in front of the class. I showed everyone a shoe box that I had covered with purple paper.

"This is the Gabby Abby mailbox," I announced. "I will put it in the coatroom. You can drop off your questions without anyone knowing! Privacy will be protected! Send me your questions and problems. Please!"

This morning when I got to school, the Gabby Abby mailbox was stuffed with questions. Hooray! Hooray! Hooray! Can't wait to read them! I hope I am wise enough to answer them all.

As the fifth-graders filed down the hall to art class, Natalie snapped candid shots with her camera.

"Don't you have enough pictures already?" Rachel asked.

"No," Natalie said. "What if none of them turns out well?" She took a picture of Mason pretending to hit Zach over the head with his math book.

"Natalie! This isn't *Life* magazine!" Jessica cried. "It's just a student newspaper!"

Natalie didn't answer. She aimed her camera at the water fountain.

" 'Conversations with Brianna' is going to be featured on the front page," Brianna bragged. She checked her watch. "Only forty-five minutes until my interview with Ms. Yang. She must be excited."

"Yay, Brianna," Bethany chirped.

"I don't know how you can stand it," Jessica muttered to Abby. "If I hear one more 'Yay, Brianna . . .' "

"Bethany's really nice when Brianna's not around," Abby whispered back. "Ignore it. That's my advice. Or write to Gabby Abby for a professional opinion."

Jessica rolled her eyes.

"Dear Gabby Abby," Zach teased. "Please advise me on how to install my new computer operating system."

"I'm answering *personal* questions," Abby said, "not offering tech support."

"Awwww!" Zach said. "Isn't my PC personal enough?"

In the art room, the new teacher was standing behind his desk. Mr. Raphael was a long-term substitute for their regular teacher, Ms. Wayne, who had left two weeks before. She was about to have a baby.

"What are we doing today?" Mason asked.

"Watercolors," Mr. Raphael announced. "Sit in your seats, and wait quietly until everyone is present."

Natalie snapped a picture of Tyler.

Mr. Raphael shook his head. "This is an art class, not a photography studio," he said to her. "Put the camera away!"

"Why can't she take photos?" Abby asked. "Class hasn't even started yet."

"No talking!" Mr. Raphael frowned at Abby. "Everyone must respect the rules!"

Abby sat down in her place. She pulled out her journal and opened it on her lap.

I wish Ms. Wayne was still teaching art instead of Mr. Raphael! I used to love art  class, but now I hate it. Mr. Raphael is too strict. His assignments are boring. We have to draw apples and bananas and oranges. Why not pineapples for a change?

Ms. Wayne is going to have her baby in the next few weeks. I wonder if it will be a boy or a girl. Will she need advice on

how to take care of it? Or maybe she
needs a name. These might be questions for
Gabby Abby! Ms. Wayne promised to visit
our class and show us the baby. Natalie
can take its picture to put in the school
newspaper.

Abby closed her journal. Mr. Raphael hadn't noticed her writing. The rule was No Talking, not No
Writing, but she didn't want to test it. Mr. Raphael
would probably say, "This is an art class, not a creative writing seminar."

He began to hand out thick, creamy paper and
boxes of watercolor paints.

"Today we are going to study a still life," he said
to the class, pointing to a table at the front of the
room.

There were plastic roses in a vase. On the table
were plastic grapes.

"Notice the patterns of light and dark," Mr.
Raphael said. "Look carefully at the shadows."

"Can't he at least use real flowers?" Jessica whispered.

"Quiet!" he ordered.

The class looked at the still life.

"If there are no questions, you may begin working now."

Abby glanced at the plastic flowers and fruit. She dipped her brush into the water and then into the pan.

"Use the whole page," Mr. Raphael said. "Don't put a small drawing in one corner."

With her brush, Abby sketched out a vase that filled the page. Big purple grapes snaked around the bottom.

"That's the idea!" Mr. Raphael said. He walked from table to table, checking each student's work.

"I'm done!" Natalie held up her watercolor. The roses were huge and dripping wet. "Can I take photos of everyone's work?"

"No!" Mr. Raphael handed Natalie another sheet of watercolor paper. "Go sit at the other side of the room and paint the still life from a new angle."

Abby secretly opened her journal again.

Poor Natalie! Now she has to do _two_ still lifes! Why are they called "still lifes"? They are not still alive; they are still plastic!

I am not going to tell Mr. Raphael that

I'm finished with my watercolor
because he'll just make me do
another one. I am going
to look at the
Gabby Abby
questions instead!

Abby took a deep breath, then slipped a question from her notebook to her lap. She unfolded the note.

"Dear Gabby Abby," she read.

"How do you get bubble gum off a T-shirt?

"Desperately yours, Sticky."

Yikes! Her first question, and she didn't have a clue how to answer it! How *do* you get bubble gum off a T-shirt? This was a question for her mother — or maybe her father, who did the laundry. She put the question aside and opened the next one.

"Dear Gabby Abby,

"I have a deep, dark secret. I am invited to a pizza party, and I am allergic to pizza. No one knows. I am too embarrassed to tell anyone! What can I do????

"Cheese Louise."

Here was a real problem! Was she up to the challenge? Abby closed her eyes and tried to imagine herself as Grandma Emma, dispensing wise, loving advice.

"I am a ten-year-old grandmother," she whispered to herself, "helping my classmates figure out the answers to their personal problems."

"Abby Hayes! What are you doing?"

With a start, Abby opened her eyes. Mr. Raphael was standing right above her. She flushed and looked down at her hands, which were covering the question. "Um, thinking about my next watercolor, Mr. Raphael."

"Get to work on it," he said abruptly.

Abby let out a long sigh of relief. That was close! What if he had seen Cheese Louise's question? What if he had read it to the class? What if he had ripped it up?

She glanced down at the question again. It wasn't a good idea to be Grandma Emma in Mr. Raphael's class. Should she imagine herself as someone else instead? Her mother, offering expensive legal advice? Isabel, dispensing facts?

As Mr. Raphael came up the aisle again, Abby quickly snatched up a brush and sketched out more grapes on a fresh sheet of paper. This time she did them in blue.

"That's the way," he said, as he passed her desk.

She put down the brush and studied the question again. She wanted to get it right. This was a serious question. She wondered whose party it was. Was Cheese Louise one of her friends? She picked up a pen and quickly wrote out an answer.

Dear Cheese Louise,
Faint when they bring the pizza in and revive when it's all eaten. No one will ever know.

Abby studied what she had written. How long would Cheese Louise have to remain unconscious? What if someone called an ambulance? What if Cheese Louise ruined the party? It would be Gabby Abby's fault! Abby scratched out what she had just written.

Dear Cheese Louise,
    Just say No, thanks to the pizza and bring a peanut butter sandwich!

There! She had done it! She had answered a question all by herself! Abby slid the next question onto her lap.

"Dear Gabby Abby,
"Why is my best friend better than me at everything?
"Discouraged."

Another serious question. Abby glanced around the room. Mr. Raphael was talking to Brianna. Jessica was at work on her third watercolor. Natalie was fiddling with the lens of her camera.

Dear Discouraged,
No one is better than everyone at everything.

Abby stopped in midsentence and thought. Who had written this letter? No one but Bethany had a best friend who was "better at everything."

You must have special talents, like taking care of animals or gymnastics. Who knows, maybe your best friend isn't so good at everything! Maybe she's just bragging!

Abby put down her pen. That should boost Bethany's confidence. She needed it, too. Jessica had a point; all those "Yay, Briannas" got on everyone's nerves. And Bethany was a really nice person, once you got to know her. Abby hoped that her letter would make a difference.

"Dear Gabby Abby,

"How do birds fly? Why is the sky blue? Why doesn't the sun go out if there's no oxygen in space?

"Curious Georgette."

Did she really have to answer this? She was an advice columnist, not an encyclopedia! Abby put it aside. Maybe the next question would be better.

"Dear Gabby Abby,

"My parents won't stop yelling. What can I do?

"Sore Ears."

This *was* a good question, but how should she answer it? She glanced again at Mr. Raphael. He was sitting at his desk, taking notes.

Dear Sore Ears,
Yell back.

No, that definitely *wasn't* good advice. Abby thought some more.

If they're not yelling at you, why don't you get earplugs?

Abby put down her pen with a sigh and unfolded the last question.

"Dear Gabby Abby,
"Why do you alweys git all the gud riting asinemints? Its no fare!
"Anonamus."

Now, how was she supposed to answer *this* one? Was it a joke? Or —
"Natalie!" Mr. Raphael's voice rang out. "If you do not put that camera away immediately, I will confiscate it!"
Slowly Natalie lowered the camera. Her face was red. "I finished two watercolors, Mr. Raphael."
He studied them. "This is unacceptable."

Abby quickly pushed the advice column papers back into her notebook. She glanced at Natalie's watercolors, then raised her hand. "Mr. Raphael, she did the assignment."

"I didn't ask for your opinion, Abby," he said.

He strode to the front of the class. "As you leave the room, hand your watercolors to me. I expect them to be signed in the lower right-hand corner, the way real artists do it."

The class gathered up their belongings and began filing out of the art room. Abby signed her watercolor in the lower left-hand corner and handed it to Mr. Raphael.

"Sorry, Natalie," Abby called as she hurried to catch up with her friend in the hallway.

She wished she had said more in Natalie's defense. She should have stood up to Mr. Raphael. Why did Natalie get picked on, anyway? She was just trying to do a good job for the newspaper. "It's really not fair!"

"I know." Natalie's head was lowered, and she clutched her camera tightly. Her shoulders slumped. "Thanks, anyway."

Gabby Abby would have had some wise words for her friend. But Abby Hayes didn't know what to do.

Chapter 7

Our tools: computers, floppy disks, a scanner, a printer, and a Xerox machine.

The job: You know what it is.

Hooray! Hooray!
We put together the newspaper today!

Is that a poem? Shall I give it to Ms. Bunder to put on the masthead?
Maybe she'd like a quote for The Lancaster Lark.
How about:

"Syllables govern the world"?
— Sir Edward Coke,
Prizewinning Pumpkin Calendar

Did Sir Edward Coke drink Pepsi? _Not_
funny!! Do not repeat this to anyone but
Dad, who loves bad jokes!

Speaking of Dad, why is he on the phone
so much lately? He looks worried all the
time. And he doesn't notice when I ask
him a question. I tried to tell him to write
to Gabby Abby, but he didn't even hear
me.

"Gabby Abby!" Ms. Bunder called from the table
where she was editing the students' articles. "I need
your column!"

"I've got it, Ms. Bunder!" Abby saved her work
onto a disk, printed out a copy, and exited the program. As she got up from her seat, Mason almost
knocked her over.

"You've been hogging that computer for *hours*,"
he said.

Abby checked her watch. "Fifteen minutes."

"Well, I have to type up my sports report," he growled, waving a piece of paper covered with red marks.

"It looks like there's not much left after editing." Natalie was scanning photographs into another computer.

Mason flushed. "If I just had to take a bunch of pictures like you, Natalie," he retorted, "my job would be *easy*!"

At another table, Jessica was working with Zach and Tyler. The masthead of the newspaper was designed and in place. Now they were working to fit the edited columns onto the page.

"We might have to cut Brianna's interview by a line or two," Jessica said. "Or else put it on page 3."

"No!" Brianna cried. "No cuts, no page 3! I'm a first-pager!" She stamped her foot angrily and stalked over to Ms. Kantor. "Tell Jessica she *can't* move me off the front page!"

Their teacher was working with Meghan on her feature article about a proposed new playground.

"Ms. Kantor!" Brianna snapped. "Did you hear me?"

"Yes, I did, Brianna. Jessica is in charge of layout. You're going to have to abide by her decision."

Brianna flounced across the room. "It's terrible how writers are treated today!"

Abby and Jessica exchanged glances.

"Put me anywhere," Abby said. Advice columns were always tucked away in the middle or at the end of a newspaper, anyway. She hoped, though, that her column wouldn't be cut too much. And that she didn't need as much editing as Mason!

"Calling Gabby Abby!" Ms. Bunder said again.

"Right here, Ms. Bunder." Abby slid into a chair next to her teacher. Her stomach began to do flip-flops. Would Ms. Bunder tell her that she had given bad advice? Would she make her rewrite all her answers?

Ms. Bunder nodded as she read the paper Abby had handed her. "Good," she said. "Very good."

Abby breathed a sigh of relief. "Really? You like it?"

"Yes, Abby. I have just one query for you. What about these?" Ms. Bunder pointed to the Curious Georgette, Anonamus, and Sticky letters.

"What about them?" Abby repeated.

"Your replies just aren't very interesting. I miss the usual Abby sparkle."

"The questions were so hard, Ms. Bunder!" she cried. "I spent *hours* looking up answers!"

For the bubble gum question, Abby had quoted from her family's *Helpful Household Hints* book.

For Curious Georgette, she had cited encyclopedia passages.

For Anonamus, she had listed all the newspaper assignments and then written, "They are all good."

"I consulted the experts!" Abby told her teacher. "Isn't that the way to do it?"

"You worked hard," Ms. Bunder acknowledged, "but I think your answers are too serious."

"Aren't they supposed to be?" Abby protested. "Isn't writing an advice column serious?"

"You don't have to play it so straight," Ms. Bunder advised her. "Be a little more daring. You can be yourself, you know."

With a frown, Abby took back the column. Be daring? Be herself? What did Ms. Bunder mean? Hadn't she been herself when she had spent an hour copying out answers to those dumb questions? And now she had to redo them!

Did the real Dear Abby get questions like "Why do you alweys git all the gud riting asinemints?"

Abby sat down at her desk and took out her purple pen. All right, she would be daring. She would be herself.

Dear Anonamus,

For one thing, I can spell. Can you? For another, what makes you think that this is such a "gud riting asinemint"? I have to answer letters like yours!

Still fuming, Abby reread the Curious Georgette questions and picked up her pen again.

Why can't Anonamus spell his or her own name? Why are you asking science questions from an advice columnist? Why are these questions so dumb?

Only one left to go. It was the bubble gum question from Sticky.

You are in a jam. (Ha-ha.) I think you're going to have to buy a new T-shirt. Next time, put your gum behind your ear.

"Is this better?" Abby asked Ms. Bunder, handing the new answers to her.

Ms. Bunder began to read.

"If you don't like it, you can use the old boring answers," Abby suggested. "Or cut the column in half. Or —"

"I think your new answers are fine," Ms. Bunder said with a smile. She handed Abby another paper. "Will you help me edit this article?" It was Bethany's science column. "Take a look at her spelling."

"Sure, Ms. Bunder." Abby stopped. "Do you really think my Gabby Abby column is okay?"

"Yes," Ms. Bunder reassured her.

"Really?" Abby asked again.

"Really!" Ms. Bunder pointed to a stack of papers. "We're under a deadline. I have to read all these columns. Yours is the least of my worries."

"Least of her worries," Abby repeated to herself as she fumbled in her backpack for a red pen. It wasn't exactly what she wanted to hear, but at least she didn't have to rewrite her answers a third time.

She turned to Bethany's article.

"This is a Sience Collum," Bethany had written, "but sinse I'm mainely intirested in anamals, I'm riting about them. Anamals are factsinating supject."

"How is it?" Bethany stood right behind her.

"Not bad," Abby said. "I'm correcting your spelling."

"I'm not very good at spelling," Bethany admitted.

"You need more practice," Abby said. "Or else a good spell-check program on the computer."

Bethany nodded. "That's what my mom says."

I just gave advice, Abby suddenly realized. *Good advice.*

It was getting easier all the time.

"Knock, knock," Rachel said, banging on the table for emphasis. She was a tall girl who liked to ski in the winter and climb mountains in the summer.

"Who's there?" Ms. Bunder asked, without looking up from the article she was editing.

"Norma Lee," Rachel said.

"Norma Lee who?"

"Norma Lee I don't go knocking on doors, but today I'm selling the best vacuum cleaner in town."

"That's lame," Bethany groaned. "I hate knock-knock jokes!"

"I like them," Abby said, handing the corrected science column to Ms. Bunder.

"Can we do a joke issue? For April Fools' Day?" Rachel asked.

"Great idea," Ms. Bunder approved.

Abby and Rachel high-fived each other.

Ms. Kantor glanced at the clock. "Come on, everybody, save your work, clean up fast! You're late for art!"

"I haven't finished!" several people wailed.

"Quick! Quick!" Ms. Kantor clapped her hands.

As the fifth-graders scrambled to clean up, Mr. Raphael poked his head in the door.

"Where's my class?"

"Sorry!" Ms. Kantor apologized. "We got so involved in our newspaper that we forgot about art! We're getting ready now!"

Mr. Raphael didn't look pleased. He stood in the doorway with his arms folded across his chest. His foot tapped impatiently on the floor.

Ms. Kantor tried to smooth things over. "We have our creative writing teacher here today for an extra hour. She's helping us with the newspaper. It's a special day. We won't be late again."

"This means less time for the clay project I planned," Mr. Raphael said.

"It's my fault," Ms. Bunder said. "It's just so exciting to put together a newspaper. Maybe you can help us with it?" she said to him.

"Perhaps," Mr. Raphael said grudgingly. "Talk to me after school."

"Mr. Raphael, I'd like to interview you for our newspaper," Brianna interrupted. She glanced at Jessica. "It'll appear on the front page."

"Maybe," Jessica warned.

Mr. Raphael frowned. "An interview?"

"A 'Conversation with Brianna,'" Brianna explained. She pulled out a pink appointment book. "What time do you have available?"

Mr. Raphael ran his fingers through his hair. "We can talk during lunch hour."

"Great!" Brianna flipped through the pages of her appointment book. "What about next Thursday?"

"Fine," Mr. Raphael agreed.

The class lined up at the door.

"Walk *quietly* to the art room," Ms. Kantor told them.

"I'll take them," Mr. Raphael said stiffly.

As the students began to file out of the classroom, Abby waved good-bye to Ms. Bunder and Ms. Kantor. "When do we finish our newspaper?" she called out to her teachers.

"Tomorrow!" Ms. Kantor promised. "At least we'll try!"

Chapter 8

Does the human mind march — or does it shuffle? In Ms. Kantor's fifth-grade class, it might even crawl!

It's taken us a <u>long</u> time to get the newspaper together. First, not everyone had their work in on time. We had trouble scanning in Natalie's photos. Some of the articles needed extra help. There were a lot of rewrites. At the last minute, Zach decided to redo his cartoons.

Today the newspaper was published. Finally!

Table of Contents

(Question: why not "Chair of Contents" or "Sofa of Contents"? Then we could sit comfortably and read . . . oh, never mind!)

Knock-knock!

In one of Natalie's photographs, Mason pretends to brain Tyler with a book. In another, Mr. Raphael is yawning. There's a close-up of Jessica about to put a spoonful of mashed potatoes into her mouth.

Early Responses to the First Edition of The Lancaster Lark

"Zach, I like the way you turned our jungle gym into a real jungle!" (Natalie, reading cartoons)

"Ha-ha-ha-ha-ha!" (Tyler and Mason, admiring their photo)

"Yay, Brianna!" (Guess who?)

"Mashed potatoes? Why not meatloaf?" (Jessica, responding to her photo)

"Of course I'm on the front page. Where else would I be?" (Guess who?)

"Gabby Abby? I can't wait to read it!" (Ms. Yang, looking at her copy.)

"Solid investigative reporting." (Ms. Kantor on Meghan's feature article about the new playground)

"Knock, knock!" (Guess who?)

Number of hamster stories in Bethany's

"Pet Tails": 4 (That was still too many! Every single one was about a hamster who escaped into a heating duct.)

Times Brianna used the words "I," "me," and "mine" in her interview with Ms. Yang: 37

Compliments Jessica got on the design and layout of the newspaper: dozens

Color Mr. Raphael's face turned when he saw his picture in the paper: dark red

"Gabby Abby" looks very different in print!

Got a cold feeling in the pit of my stomach when I reread the questions and answers.

Are Anonamus and Curious Georgette going to be mad at me? I told them their questions were stupid! I told Sticky to stick his gum behind his ear!! What will they  think? What was _I_ thinking???? My answers don't sparkle, they crackle and pop! They explode!! I should have been more tactful and polite, even though the questions <u>were</u> stupid!

Ms. Bunder, why didn't you stop me??!!!
My first answers wouldn't have offended
anyone! (She was right, though. They were
pretty boring.)

I'm glad I'm on page 4! Maybe no one
will read my column? No one will notice
rude advice?

The other answers were better. Advised
Cheese Louise to bring a peanut butter
sandwich to the party. Pointed out to Discouraged that her best friend was probably
bragging and also mentioned that she was
better at diving and gymnastics than her
friend. Told Sore Ears to wear earplugs
when his or her parents yell.

I think I did okay . . . at least part
of the time.

Resolutions

Next time be more patient with stupid
questions!

Concentrate on real problems; give best advice.
Don't worry; be happy!

Went home in good mood. Ran up to

Dad's office to show him newspaper. As usual in the past few weeks, he was on the phone. He ignored me when I waved the paper at him.

I decided to go downstairs to show Alex instead. My little brother enjoyed Rachel's knock-knock jokes. He said my column was the best in the newspaper. Alex and I played a game of cards together. Then he asked me to look at a new computer game that he had just gotten.

"What's wrong with Dad lately?" I asked him while the program was booting up. "He's always worried about something. He doesn't listen when I talk to him."

Alex frowned. "Last night I heard Mom and Dad talking about a nursing home. I heard them mention Grandma Emma."

My heart began to pound. "Is something wrong with Grandma Emma?"

"I don't know," Alex said. "I fell asleep after that."

When we all went on vacation, Grandma Emma was very healthy. She had more energy than most of us. Mom took a nap every day, but not Grandma Emma. We walked and climbed and hiked all day long. She never complained about being tired or sick.

"Excuse me, Alex," I said. "I'll look at your game later. I <u>have</u> to talk to Dad!"

I ran up the stairs. As I burst into the room, Dad hung up the phone. He started to dial another number.

"Dad!" I cried. "What's going on? Is Grandma Emma sick? I have to know! Tell me everything!"

For a moment, Dad looked at me as if he didn't recognize me. Then he put down the phone. "Don't worry, Abby. Your grandma is fine."

"What's wrong, then?" I asked, sitting down in a chair. My heart was thudding like crazy. I couldn't get it to calm down.

"It's your great-uncle Jack. He can't take care of himself anymore. Your mother and I are trying to find an assisted living situation for him. He needs meals, rides to doctors' appointments, and help taking medication. It's very difficult because he doesn't want to admit he needs help."

"You're <u>sure</u> nothing's wrong with Grandma Emma?" I demanded.

"She's fine," my father reassured me. He rubbed his hand over his unshaven chin. "She's worried about Great-uncle Jack, just like the rest of us."

PHEW!!!!!!!!!! I let out my breath. Even though I was sorry Great-uncle Jack couldn't take care of himself anymore, I was GLAD it wasn't Grandma Emma.

I don't know Great-uncle Jack very well, but Dad said that he was very good to Mom when she was going to law school. Dad said that Great-uncle Jack has a very independent nature and that it's hard for him to get old.

Then Dad and I had a long conversation. He said he was sorry he hadn't paid much attention to me lately. He said he and Mom wanted to find the right situation for Great-uncle Jack and that took a lot of time and telephone calls.

I ran downstairs for <u>The Lancaster Lark</u> and showed him my column. He laughed at Natalie's photographs and at my response

to Sticky. (Maybe Sticky <u>won't</u> be mad?)
He thought Gabby Abby was a great name.
He promised to finish reading my column af-
ter dinner.

"Why not right now?" I asked.

Dad checked his watch. "I'd love to, but
I have to contact the director of a facility
before her office closes."

He sighed, gave me a quick hug, and
reached for the phone.

As I was writing this, Natalie called.

"Your pictures are great!" I cried. "Aren't
you happy?"

"They could have been a lot better."

"What?????" I said. "My dad loved
them. So did I. So did a lot of people."

Natalie didn't answer. Instead, she told
me an astonishing and shocking fact. She is
Discouraged.

"<u>You</u> wrote the letter about the best friend
who's better at everything than you?" I
gasped.

"Yes," Natalie said.

"No!" I cried.

We both fell silent for a moment.

"Do you mean it?" I burst out. "Are you really discouraged by me? Or is it Jessica?"

"I'm jealous of both of you," Natalie confessed. "I just rolled it up into one question."

"Why? Why are you jealous?" I asked.

"New kid in town," Natalie muttered. "I don't know."

"I can't believe this!" I said. "You act in plays! You solve mysteries! You do chemistry experiments! You take photos!"

"I guess."

"I'm jealous of you!" I cried.

Natalie laughed shakily. "I never thought of it that way."

I wanted to remind Natalie of how she read more books than anyone in the fifth grade. That she was the best actress in the class — better even than Brianna. And that if anyone figured out how to turn rocks into diamonds and gold, it would be her.

But, suddenly, I realized what I had done.

"Oh, no!" I cried. "I told Discouraged that her best friend was bragging. I told her that she was good at gymnastics and taking care of animals."

My face was hot. "When Brianna reads the letter, she'll think it's about her!"

I stopped to think about it. "She'll fight with Bethany. Their friendship will end! Bethany will end _our_ friendship! How could I have been so stupid?"

Natalie tried to reassure me. "Brianna and Bethany probably won't even read the column."

"Wrong! They will!" I insisted. "Or someone else will tell them!"

"You can apologize," Natalie suggested.

"Will they accept it?" I cried. "And what will it be like, saying 'I'm sorry' to Brianna?"

I was so upset about Bethany and Brianna that I hung up without saying anything about the most important problem of all: Natalie. I wish she was Encouraged, not Discouraged!

It's hard to believe that she is envious of me and Jessica. She is envious of _our_ talents when she has so many of her own. I still can't get over it!

I should have noticed that she wasn't very confident about her photography. She thinks her pictures are no good. She's wrong!

And she doesn't realize what a good actress she is. Or what a good friend she is. Who cares if she's the new kid in town?

Must try to build up Natalie's confidence. Will publish Gabby Abby's Seven Secrets of Self-Esteem. (Problem: What _are_ Gabby Abby's Seven Secrets of Self-Esteem?)

Gabby Abby's
Seven Secrets
of
Self-Esteem

P.S. I am going to need Gabby Abby's Seven Secrets of Self-Esteem if Bethany and Brianna are mad at me!

Think fast! Help Natalie. Help myself. Help! Help! HELP!!!!!!

Chapter 9

Thursday

"Whatever you lose, reckon
of no account."

— *Publius Syrus*

Piggy Bank Calendar

Oh, yeah? What about my friendship
with Bethany? Is that "of no account"? I
will be very sad if our friendship is over.

And what about Natalie? She <u>has</u> lost
confidence in herself. She has to get it
back!

Must find a better quote! I opened the
Happy Days Calendar and saw this:

"Cheer up; the worst is yet to come."
— <u>Philander Chase Johnson</u>

Help! Is this an omen? Forget about inspiring quotes! Will fortify self with break-fast cereal, instead.

As Abby entered the school yard, she saw Bethany and Brianna talking together near the slide. Her heart began to pound.

"Chin up," Abby told herself. "Stand straight and tall. Face the music."

She wished it *was* music she had to face! She didn't feel very confident or strong. Was this how Natalie felt all the time?

Taking deep breaths of air to calm herself, she went up to the two girls.

"Uh, hi, Bethany. Hi, Brianna."

"Guess what?" Bethany smiled at her as if nothing had happened. "My mom and dad liked 'Pet Tails'! They were amazed at the good spelling. I told them you helped me, Abby!"

"I-I did," Abby stuttered. "I mean, you're welcome. Anytime." She looked down at her hands.

"My mom said the hamster stories were true to life," Bethany continued. "My dad said they were gripping and dramatic."

Brianna made a bored gesture. "Enough about hamsters."

"Oh — and I almost forgot! 'Gabby Abby' was a hoot," Bethany said.

Abby stared at her. "A hoot?" she repeated. "As in owl hooting?"

Bethany giggled. "You're funny! Just like Gabby Abby. I loved what you wrote to Anonamus and Curious Georgette. My parents said you have a great sense of humor."

"They did? I do?"

Brianna interrupted. "Today my father is distributing copies of my interview with Ms. Yang to all his coworkers," she bragged. "He says if there were a Pulitzer Prize for kids' reporting, I'd get it!"

Abby ignored her. "You read my *entire* column?" she asked Bethany in disbelief.

"Sure," Bethany said. "Then I put it in Blondie's cage. Blondie nibbled it."

Brianna interrupted again. "Ms. Yang wrote me a thank-you note for the interview," she announced. "She loves having contact with gifted students like me. It's the most satisfying part of her job."

"She actually said that?" Abby asked.

"That's what she *meant*," Brianna said. "I can read between the lines."

Abby took a deep breath. "Did you read my column, too?"

"I saw it," Brianna said. "It was on the last page."

"Are you mad?"

"Mad?" Brianna looked at her as if she were crazy. "I got front-page placement AND my picture in the paper. Of course I'm not mad."

The first bell rang. Abby stood in line, waiting to be let into the school. Someone tapped her shoulder. She turned and saw Mason and Zach grinning at her.

"Way to go, Gabby Abby!" Mason burped three times in a row. "Mason Man liked it!"

"Great column!" Zach said.

"Really??" Abby said.

Out of the corner of her eye, Abby saw Natalie hurrying toward the school. She waved wildly. Natalie didn't respond.

"Hi, Gabby Abby!" a second-grader called out.

"I think you should call the column 'Crabby Abby,' " Jonathan said. He carried a clarinet case in one hand and a hockey stick in the other. "Because you get mad at almost everyone who writes you a letter."

"That's good!" Mason yelled. "Crabby Abby, the Annoyed Adviser!"

"That's one name I didn't think of," Abby admitted.

"It was funny!" Meghan whispered, pushing a strand of hair out of her face.

"Guess who Anonamus is?" Zach asked.

"A great speller?" Abby teased.

Mason and Zach punched each other. "It's us!" They yelled. "We wrote it as a joke!"

"Ha-ha-ha," Abby said. "Very amusing."

As they passed the school office, Ms. Bunder emerged with a pile of books in her arms.

"The first issue is a great success!" she said. "I'm so proud of you all!" Then she complimented each student individually.

"Clever cartoons," she said to Zach. "Thought-provoking article," she said to Meghan. "Good jokes," she said to Rachel.

"Gabby Abby was sparkling and lively," she said to Abby.

"Um, yes," Abby said. She felt dizzy. She had expected everyone to be angry, but they were pleased instead. It didn't make sense.

Abby entered the coatroom and hung up her jacket and hat. She unfastened her boots and got out her sneakers. She hoped Natalie would show up soon. She wanted to talk to her.

"I'm interviewing Mr. Raphael today," Brianna announced as she took off a white plush coat to reveal a blue cap-sleeve dress underneath. "I hope he appreciates his luck. He'll be on the front page with me."

"You're not guaranteed a spot on page 1!" Jessica pulled off her boots and put on her sneakers. "Your next interview might even end up on the last page!"

"No!" Brianna cried indignantly.

"Yes!" Jessica took her binder from her backpack. "Don't make promises you can't keep."

Brianna opened her mouth, then closed it. She grabbed her homework and flounced out of the room.

"You told her!" Abby gave Jessica a thumbs-up sign. "Way to go!"

Jessica grinned.

"She probably *will* end up on the front page again," Jessica confessed in a whisper. "Ms. Kantor wants to spotlight the teacher interviews. But I'm not telling Brianna that!"

Out of the corner of her eye, Abby saw Natalie standing alone at the coatroom door.

"Natalie!" Abby cried. "Join us!"

Did Natalie realize how much her friends appreciated her? If she did, she wouldn't feel so Discouraged. But before Abby could utter a word, Natalie disappeared into the classroom.

Abby opened her desk. On top of her books was an envelope addressed to Gabby Abby. She opened it. Inside was a plain piece of lined paper. The letter was written in pencil.

"Dear Gabby Abby,

"I took your advice about the earplugs. I didn't hear as much yelling, but I also didn't hear my mom and dad calling me for dinner, or asking me to take out the garbage, or telling me to turn off the computer. Boy, were they mad! Then I heard a lot more yelling than usual. Plus my computer got shut off for a week. What do I do now?

"Very Sore Ears."

As Abby stared at the message in dismay, Meghan tapped her on the shoulder.

"What is it?" Without looking up, she opened her binder and took out her homework assignment.

"I'm Cheese Louise," Meghan whispered.

"Yes?"

"You told me to bring a peanut butter sandwich to the party. Well, I'm even more allergic to peanut butter than cheese. If I eat it, I can die."

"Oh!" Abby groaned.

"I just wanted you to know," Meghan whispered. She tiptoed away.

Chapter 10

<u>True!</u> One puny sword (even a sharp one) could never match the mighty wrath of Cabby Abby's purple pen!

(Why am I making jokes? This is NOT funny!!!)

<u>Damage Done by Cabby Abby's Pen</u>

1. Sore Ears is now Very Sore Ears. He lost computer privileges for a week.

2. Natalie is avoiding me.

3. <u>If</u> Bethany finds out that I thought she was Discouraged, she will be mad at me.

4. Ditto for Brianna.

5. I would have killed Meghan — if she had taken my advice. (Fortunately, she knew about her peanut butter allergy. Unfortunately, she still doesn't know what to do at the party.)

6. Friendships ended. Parents angered. Happiness shattered!

7. Ruin, destruction, misery!!!!!!

Damage Done by Sharp Sword

1. None.

Humanity Uplifted by Gabby Abby's Pen

1. Half a dozen people laughed. One smirked. A few were amused.

(Is this good enough? No!!!!)

Quick Report on Breakfast Conversation in the Hayes Family Kitchen

Me: Mom, can I be sued for bad advice?

Mom (drinking first cup of coffee): Unnnhh?

Me: This is a legal question. Can Gabby

Abby be sued for damages to friendships and family relationships?

Mom (confused): Gabby Abby???

Me: My advice column.

Mom: Your _what_???

Me: My advice has messed up one kid's life, and it almost killed someone else. It would have been death by peanut butter.

Mom (chokes on her coffee at this confession).

Dad (interrupts): Your mom and I were up very late last night talking about Great-uncle Jack. Why don't you save it for another time, Abby?

Me: Okay, but I need to know soon.

Now that my pen has wreaked havoc in the world, what do I do? Resign from the column? Hide under the bed for a week? Quit the human race????

"We're going to start the second issue of the newspaper today," Ms. Kantor announced first thing Friday morning.

"I just can't win!" Abby put her head down on her desk.

Brianna waved her hand in the air. "Ms. Kantor! I'm already writing up my interview with Mr. Raphael. He told me all about his studies in Italy. He said I should go there someday."

"And she should stay there, too," Jessica whispered to Abby.

"How do you say 'I am the best' in Italian?" Abby murmured. She glanced over at Natalie to see if she had heard.

Natalie was scribbling a chemical formula in a notebook.

"Pssst!" Abby said. "Natalie!"

Natalie didn't respond.

"What's the matter with her?" Jessica whispered.

"I don't know," Abby lied. "Maybe she's thinking about her photos." She wished she could confide in Jessica, but she couldn't reveal that Discouraged was Natalie. Didn't advice columnists have to keep people's identities secret?

"I want to do more 'Pet Tails,'" Bethany said. "I have *loads* more hamster stories!"

"Maybe you can focus on other animals," Ms. Kantor suggested.

"Write about my horse, Winter Star," Brianna told Bethany. "You can tell how I was first in the riding competition last spring."

Abby raised her hand.

"Yes, Abby?" Ms. Kantor said.

"May I please be excused from writing another advice column?" she said.

"Keep Gabby Abby!" Zach pleaded. "She's funny!"

"I wasn't trying to be funny," Abby explained to Ms. Kantor. "I didn't want anyone to laugh."

Or get yelled at, or have allergic reactions, or feel embarrassed or resentful, she added silently.

"Then don't *try* to be funny!" Mason yelled. "You're more hilarious that way!"

"Mason! Calm down!" Ms. Kantor scolded.

"You're not excused," she said to Abby. "Don't you see that you have a fan club already?"

Abby groaned.

"Continue what you started. You may even find you like it." Ms. Kantor smiled. "I thought you did a pretty good job, Abby."

Some of the boys and a few of the girls applauded.

Abby glanced over at Natalie. She was still writing in her notebook.

"Any other questions?" Ms. Kantor asked.

Brianna stood up. "Ms. Kantor, yesterday I interviewed Mr. Raphael during lunch hour."

"Yes, Brianna, we know."

"He was very upset, Ms. Kantor, by Natalie's portrayal of him in the newspaper. He said it was disrespectful and rude."

"What's wrong with showing a teacher yawning?" Abby jumped to her feet to defend Natalie's work.

With a frown, Natalie looked up from her notebook.

"It shows him being tired!" Brianna said indignantly. "Or bored!"

"So?" Abby said.

"It's not — dignified!" Brianna explained.

"At least you didn't take a picture of Mr. Raphael picking his nose," Abby whispered to Natalie.

Natalie almost smiled.

"He wants approval of any picture of him that appears in *The Lancaster Lark*," Brianna concluded. "He doesn't want Natalie to take any more pictures of him."

"I'll do a cartoon for the interview!" Zach offered.

"This brings up some good questions." Ms. Kantor got up from her desk. "What do you think, class?

Do you think the picture was disrespectful? A show of hands if you agree."

Brianna's hand shot up in the air. Several others joined her. Bethany raised her hand, lowered it, and then raised it again.

"We have five people who think this photo is disrespectful. What about the rest of you?"

"No!" a dozen kids yelled out.

"Raise your hands, not your voices!" Ms. Kantor reminded them. She counted the hands and announced, "Nineteen kids think this photo is fine. Now let's hear from the photographer. Natalie? Stand up, please."

Natalie ran her fingers through her already tousled hair and stood up. She looked around nervously.

"What's your opinion, Natalie?" Ms. Kantor asked. "Why did you take this photograph, and what were you trying to show?"

"I wasn't trying to show anything," Natalie muttered. "I wasn't trying to be rude or disrespectful, either. It was just a picture of someone yawning. It happened to be a teacher. I took a picture of Jessica eating and a picture of Mason and Tyler pretending to have a fight. They were all things that happened during the school day."

"So you were showing moments of the school day," Ms. Kantor said.

"Yes," Natalie agreed. She sat down in her seat.

"Does this change anyone's opinion?" Ms. Kantor asked.

Bethany looked around. Then she slowly raised her hand.

"Bethany? What do you think?"

Bethany flushed a deep red. "I think the picture is okay," she whispered.

"No, it isn't!" Brianna glared at her.

Ms. Kantor turned to Brianna. "Everyone is entitled to an opinion, Brianna. If Mr. Raphael doesn't want Natalie to take his picture, then he won't have his photo in the paper. But we're not going to stop printing her photos. I think most of the class agrees. Now, are there any more questions?"

She glanced around the room. "None? Okay, let's get to work!"

Abby got up to check the advice column mailbox.

"Way to go, Natalie," she said as she passed her friend.

"Yeah," Natalie mumbled. "Thanks." She ducked her head and began to sort through a pile of photos on her desk.

Abby walked away. It was too late now to say anything more. She could have pointed out how good Natalie's pictures were. Abby could have said that *The Lancaster Lark* needed more, not fewer of Natalie's photos!

She had once again missed an opportunity to help her friend.

Chapter 11

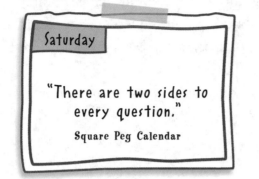

Saturday

"There are two sides to every question."

Square Peg Calendar

How many sides are there to every answer? There were six questions in the Gabby Abby mailbox yesterday. Some were silly, some were serious.

If each answer has two sides, that means twelve answers in all.

TO: Gabby Abby

Being an advice columnist is a lot of responsibility. Can I do it? I <u>want</u> to do it!

At least I think I do.

<u>Gabby Abby Resolutions</u>

1. Do NOT make anyone mad, upset, embarrassed, or confused.

2. Do NOT try to figure out who wrote the letters. Do NOT jump to conclusions. (Note: Why do people jump to conclusions? Why not slide, stumble, or bump into them? I will NOT bump into any more conclusions when writing Gabby Abby!)

3. Do NOT give dangerous, fatal advice.

4. Answer all questions with simple words: Yes, No, and I don't know.

5. "Speak softly and carry a big stick?" (A president of the United States, Teddy Roosevelt, said that. Did he write an advice column, too? What was the big stick for? To protect him from people who didn't like his advice?)

I'm glad it's Saturday. I'm going to do something this weekend that has nothing to do with newspapers, advice columns, or personal problems!

"What's for dinner?" Abby asked as she entered the

kitchen, stamping her feet on the mat. "It smells good."

"Take those wet boots off," her father ordered. "Eva just mopped the floor."

"Okay, Dad." Abby had just come from Heather's house. Heather was a grad student who lived a few houses away. She had brown hair that was wild and curly like Abby's. She made her own sweaters and spoke Spanish and English.

Heather had paid her five dollars to staple and fold a big stack of papers. When she was done stapling and folding, Abby had played with Heather's cat, Marshmallow.

Her father chopped a tomato and scraped it into a bowl. Bowls of olives, peppers, and grated cheese were scattered on the counter.

"I'm making pizza," he said. "That's the onions you smell cooking."

"Yum!"

Her father had a worried line between his eyes. "Have you seen your mother?" he said.

"She went out shopping with Isabel a while ago. She said she'd be back for dinner." Abby hung her coat on the peg near the door.

"Heather taught me some Spanish words. *Consejo.* That means advice. *Uno, dos, tres, quatro, cinco, seis, siete, ocho, nueve, diez*," Abby recited. "That's counting to ten. Heather has exams in a week and then she has a month off! I wish I was in college!"

"Mmmm," her father said. He barely missed slicing his finger with the knife.

"Watch out, Dad," Abby said. "Your head is in the clouds." That's what her grandmother said when someone wasn't paying attention.

Her father barely responded. He poured sauce over the pizza crust and then sprinkled cheese, tomatoes, onions, and peppers over the top. "Why don't you set the table?" he said.

"Okay." Abby took the silverware and napkins from the drawer and brought them over to the table. She folded the napkins and put one at each place.

There were footsteps on the back porch.

"I found five new colors of nail polish," Isabel announced triumphantly as she came through the door, laden with packages.

"And we both bought new winter boots," her mother added.

Paul Hayes slid the pizza in the oven. He set down

the pot holder. "I just got another call," he said, with a meaningful glance at his wife. "We need to talk."

Olivia Hayes nodded. She hung up her coat and turned to Isabel. "Please get the rest of the packages out of the car."

She headed toward the living room. Paul Hayes untied his chef's apron and hurried after her.

"What's that all about?" Isabel said to Abby.

"Probably Great-uncle Jack." Abby placed forks on the folded napkins.

"Sure. But what now?"

Abby shrugged. "I don't know." She could hear the murmuring of her parents' voices from the other room.

Isabel went out to the car to retrieve the packages. She let the door bang loudly behind her.

Abby got the dishes from the cupboard and set them around the table. Whatever her parents had to worry about, she hoped it wouldn't involve her. She had a column to write and Natalie to worry about. Wasn't that enough for any ten-year-old?

"The pizza almost burned," Olivia Hayes observed, cutting off a particularly dark section of crust from her slice.

Homemade pizza had just been served. The entire family was sitting around the table.

"It's well done," her husband said. "Fortunately Isabel caught it just in time."

"It was Abby who noticed the burning smell," Isabel pointed out.

"Hooray, Abby," Alex cheered. Tomato sauce was already smeared on his mouth and T-shirt.

"Good teamwork, Abby and Isabel," their mother said.

Eva checked her watch. "Speaking of teamwork, I have practice in half an hour."

Paul Hayes put down his fork. "Don't leave yet, Eva. We have something to discuss with you," he said.

Abby shifted in her seat. Whenever her parents had "something to discuss," it was usually not pleasant.

"Is this what you were talking about in the living room?" Isabel demanded.

Their father nodded.

Olivia Hayes cleared her throat. "As you know, your great-uncle Jack can't take care of himself anymore," she began. "We've finally found a place for him to live, but now someone has to move him out of his apartment and into the assisted-care facility."

"A mover?" Alex suggested.

"It's too much for Great-uncle Jack to pack and unpack by himself. He needs his family to help," their father explained. "Your mother and I will take care of the move for him."

Their mother nodded. "We'll take a week off, fly there, clean out his apartment, set up his new quarters, and then come back. Obviously, this is going to disrupt all of our lives."

"Will it interfere with my drama rehearsals?" Isabel asked.

"What about my games?" Eva demanded.

"Who's going to take care of us?" Abby asked. "Grandma Emma?" she said hopefully.

Paul Hayes sighed. "That's the problem. Grandma Emma can't come. We don't know what to do."

Isabel and Eva jumped up from their seats. "Leave us in charge!" they cried out in unison. "We'll cook dinner, get rides from our friends, and make sure Abby does her math homework."

Alex and Abby looked at each other. The twins in charge? For an entire week? "No way!" they yelled.

"Eva and Isabel are *much* too young to be responsible for a household for a week," Olivia Hayes said.

"Absolutely not."

Abby and Alex sighed with relief.

"What about our friends?" Alex asked. "Can we stay with them?"

"Yes!" Eva agreed.

"Great idea, Alex!" Isabel said.

Abby didn't respond. She didn't want to be away from home for a week, even at Jessica's house.

And what about T-Jeff? Who'd take care of him while they were gone? He'd be lonely!

"How many families could take one or more of you for a week?" Olivia Hayes asked. "We'd disrupt their lives and yours. It'd be a lot easier if we could find someone to stay here with you."

"Yes!" Abby cried.

"But who?" Paul Hayes asked. "We need someone *now*. We were lucky to find an opening for your great-uncle Jack in an excellent facility. Your mother and I have to leave within two weeks."

No one said anything.

"Any other ideas?" Olivia Hayes asked, after a moment. "Is there another way to do this?"

"We have an advice columnist in the family," Isabel said jokingly. "Maybe we should ask her."

"Come on, Gabby Abby," Eva teased. "Give us your wise advice."

"I'm not that great at giving advice," Abby protested, and then stopped. She didn't have to let her family know that she was the world's worst advice columnist. Even if she were the best, they'd never take her seriously, anyway. They'd laugh her advice off. She might as well deliberately try to make everyone laugh.

"Gabby Abby says . . . Gabby Abby says . . . " She tried to think of something really funny, but what came out of her mouth was, "Get Heather to stay with us!"

Chapter 12

Saturday still

"Great thoughts come from the heart."

—Marquis de Vauvenargues

Thunder and Lightning Calendar

My great thought about Heather <u>might</u> have come from my heart. But it might also have come from my throat, nose, elbow, or fingertips.

Who cares where it came from? I know where it went! Right into the heads and hearts of my family who cheered and applauded my suggestion.

<u>News Flash! From Your Secret Star Reporter, Abby Hayes!</u>

(Note: This is NOT <u>The Lancaster Lark!</u>

This is Abby Hayes, and I am the chief investigative reporter, feature editor, and newsroom manager. I am also the humor columnist and sports reporter!)

Abby Hayes's brilliant suggestion to ask their neighbor Heather to stay with the Hayes siblings was met with universal re-joicing. After the Hayes family had finished congratulating Abby on her outstanding ad-vice, Olivia Hayes got on the phone to Heather. Within five minutes, Heather was at the Hayes house, sitting at the dining room table with a slice of almost-burned homemade pizza and a glass of cider in front of her.

Paul Hayes opened the discussion. "We need to go out of town for a week to deal with a family emergency. Will you stay at the house with the kids?"

Eva and Isabel Hayes immediately protested that they were no longer kids! Abby Hayes said she was practically a teenager. Alex Hayes said he would be a teenager one day, even though he was only in second grade now.

"Okay, will you stay with our offspring?" Paul Hayes corrected himself.

"Excuse me." Eva stood up. "I'm late for basketball practice. Dad, I need a ride."

After this untimely interruption, the discussion continued. Heather indicated her willingness to stay at the Hayes household. She has a driver's license and can take everyone to practices, rehearsals, meetings, and friends' houses. She can also shop, cook, and help with homework.

Olivia Hayes said they would pay her for the week. Heather said the extra money would come in handy for the holidays. She wants to buy expensive hand-dyed yarn to make a jacket for her mother.

Now the Hayes parents are arranging their trip. The Hayes offspring are happy. Isabel likes Heather because she has traveled all over the world. Eva likes Heather because she played softball in high school. Alex likes Heather because she asks him about his robots. Abby likes Heather be-

cause she gave her T-Jeff. (And for a lot
of other reasons!)

Heather plans to bring her cat, Marshmallow, to the Hayes house while she is there.
Marshmallow will have a reunion with her
son, T-Jeff! The Secret Star Reporter asked
the frisky kitten how he felt about this.
T-Jeff responded by meowing loudly.

Mini-News Flash!

Still stunned that no one had laughed at
her advice and thrilled by the enthusiastic
response of her family, Abby Hayes sat
down to answer the Gabby Abby questions.
Suddenly, she noticed that something unusual
had happened. The questions didn't look as
difficult as they had earlier in the day.
Abby no longer felt so afraid of giving bad
answers. She no longer felt that she had to
answer Yes, No, or Maybe to every question.

"After all," she said to T-Jeff, who had
jumped into her lap and was purring in
agreement, "if my answers were so terrible
the first time, why did anyone write back
to me????"

The fifth-grade advice columnist is now opening the first envelope!

"Dear Gabby Abby,
"I want a scooter, but my parents won't buy one for me. What can I do?
"Scootless."

Dear Scootless,
  I can't believe you're writing to me. Do you have a piggy bank? Do you know how to rake leaves and shovel snow? Can you baby-sit or dog walk? DUH!!!!

"Dear Gabby Abby,
"I like yur columm. Its funnie.
"Gess Hoo."

Thenks, Zak and Maysen. Or is it sumwon ilse?

"Dear Gabby Abby,
"Someone is steeling disserts from my backpack. Help!
"Disserted."

Dear Disserted,

This is a serious problem, especially if you like desserts better than sandwiches. I think you should bring gooey, chocolatey desserts to school until you find out who has the stickiest fingers!

"Dear Gabby Abby,

"When I grow up, I want to become an advice columnist just like you!

"Eager Edgar."

Dear Eager Edgar,

Yes, you can be an advice columnist, too! Just practice telling people what to do, thinking up silly answers to silly questions, and solving personal problems. Anyone can do it!

P.S. When you least expect it, kids will get mad at your advice. Also when you least expect it, they <u>won't</u> get mad at your advice.

But don't worry! Have fun! Just don't tell people to eat peanut butter sandwiches or to wear earplugs.

Abby reread Sore Ears's question.

"Dear Gabby Abby,

"I took your advice about the earplugs. I didn't hear as much yelling, but I also didn't hear my mom and dad calling me for dinner, or asking me to take out the garbage, or telling me to turn off the computer. Boy, were they mad! Then I heard a lot more yelling than usual. Plus my computer got shut off for a week. What do I do now?

"Very Sore Ears."

Dear Sore Ears,
"Smile and the world smiles with you." That's what my mother says. Try it! No one can get mad at you if you smile.

"Dear Gabby Abby,

"What can I do? I told a friend some personal things about myself, and now I'm too embarrassed to talk to her.

"Pinkie."

Dear Pinkie,
I am not going to guess who wrote this

letter. Even though I <u>know</u> who wrote this
letter. All I have to say is DON'T
WORRY! Your friend still likes you!

Abby put down her pen, then picked it up again.

<u>Tiny News Flash</u>
Abby Hayes has just finished the
second Gabby Abby column! The weary
but happy advice columnist wipes her brow
in relief. Hooray! She gets up to call
her friend Natalie and invite her over
tomorrow.
If she has solved a complicated Hayes
family problem, why can't she help Natalie,
too? She can, she can, she <u>can!</u>

<u>Itty-Bitty News Flash</u>
Natalie won't come to the phone. She
doesn't want to talk. Abby Hayes hangs
up in defeat.

<u>Microscopically Small News Flash</u>
After five minutes, Abby Hayes calls

back. Why won't Natalie talk to her?

Itty-Bitty Eensy-Weensy News Flash
She calls back again. Natalie <u>has</u> to talk to her.

Almost Invisible News Flash
Abby won't stop until Natalie talks to her.
She calls again.
   And again.
      And again..
         And again.

Huge, Gigantic, Breakthrough News Flash!
Natalie has decided to speak to Abby Hayes. She is on her way to the phone right now.

Chapter 13

Saturday still

"All things come to those who wait."

Airport Calendar

And to those who call. I called Natalie seven times before she agreed to talk to me. I am now waiting for "all things" to come to me.

Abby clutched the phone tightly to her ear. She could hear footsteps in the background and the voices of Natalie's family.

"Okay, okay," Natalie said. "I'm getting it. All *right*?" She picked up the phone. "Hello?"

"Hi, Pinkie!" Abby blurted out. Then she clapped her hand to her forehead. She had done it again! What if Pinkie was Bethany? Or Brianna? Or

Rachel? Or Meghan? Or even Zach or Tyler or Mason?

There was a short silence at the other end of the line. Then Natalie giggled.

Abby sighed with relief. "I knew it!"

"I hoped you would figure it out," Natalie admitted.

"You did? Why wouldn't you talk to me sooner? Why did you make me call seven times?"

"I felt stupid. And embarrassed. And —" Natalie stopped. "I don't know!"

"You're *not* stupid!" Abby protested.

"Yes, I am!"

"You are not."

"I *am*!"

"Natalie!" Abby cried. "It isn't true!"

Natalie didn't reply.

Abby searched desperately for the perfect words to say to her friend. Should she begin by reassuring her that her friends loved her? By complimenting her on her talents? By telling Natalie to trust her friends? The words crowded in her head.

In the end, all she could manage was, "Are you mad at me?"

"I'm not," Natalie mumbled. "I'm sorry I've been

sort of, well —" Her voice trailed off. "It's just —"

Abby waited.

"You and Jessica are so good at *everything*!" Natalie burst out. "It's not easy to be your friend!"

"Are you serious?"

"Haven't you noticed that the whole class loves Gabby Abby?" Natalie cried. "Everyone but Brianna reads it over and over."

"So?" Abby shifted uncomfortably. "It's just one column. And I made lots of mistakes! Really awful ones."

"No one noticed," Natalie said. "They all loved it! Everyone always loves your writing! And they all love Jessica's designs and drawings!"

"But you — you —" Abby stuttered.

"I just click a camera button, and I get in trouble with Mr. Raphael," Natalie said. "It's not hard."

"That's not true!" Abby protested. "You experiment with chemistry, you read books, you —"

Natalie cut her off. "Stop, Abby."

"But think of all you do!" Abby cried.

"Why?" Natalie said. "It'll just make me feel worse."

"I can't believe you!" Abby said. "Do you know how crazy this is?"

"Crazy?" Natalie repeated slowly. "I'm crazy, too?"

"I didn't mean it that way!" Abby cried. This was one of the most frustrating conversations she'd ever had. Everything she said seemed to get twisted around. She didn't know how to untwist it, either.

"I know you're trying to be nice to me," Natalie conceded.

"No, I'm not!" Abby protested. "I'm telling you the truth!"

Natalie didn't say anything.

There was nothing more to say.

Saying good-bye to Natalie, Abby hung up the phone. She glanced at the Airport Calendar and the quote of the day.

" 'All things come to those who wait,' " she read out loud.

She picked up her journal and began to write.

That quote didn't say what things come to those who wait! It didn't say whether they were good or bad.

Good Things That Came to Me
1. Natalie is talking to me again.

2. Natalie told me what was bothering her.

3. Natalie gave me lots of compliments about my column.

Bad Things That Came to Me

1. Natalie doesn't believe that she is much good at anything.

2. Natalie won't listen when I try to tell her she is.

3. Natalie is still Discouraged!

P.S. I am Discouraged, too. I can't seem to help my friend. What can I do?

P.P.S. I didn't wait for an answer to my parents' problem! Why do I have to wait for an answer for Natalie?

Chapter 14

New strength and new thoughts <u>didn't</u> come with the new day. They didn't show up until halfway through the morning.

<u>News Flash! Abby Hayes Has Brainstorm in Ms. Bunder's Class!</u>

On Thursday morning, the fifth-grade advice columnist was hit by the brainstorm of the century. It began innocently. The second issue of <u>The Lancaster Lark</u> had just come out. Ms. Bunder asked the students for their ideas for a third issue.

Meghan raised her hand and said that

she wanted to write an article about next week's theater workshop. Bethany asked if she could profile the local animal shelter. Zach plans to draw cartoon portraits of the school staff. Rachel announced that she would switch from knock-knock jokes to light-bulb jokes...

Only Abby Hayes was silent. As the advice columnist, she did not need to think of a new idea. All she had to do was answer the questions in the Gabby Abby mailbox. When she checked that morning, there were twelve new questions!

Brianna stood up. The fifth-grader most likely to become a television anchorwoman announced that she would interview the music teacher for the next "Conversations with Brianna." Reading from a slip of paper, Brianna said that she planned to write a song in honor of the teacher.

Ms. Kantor approved the idea. "It's important to spotlight our teachers," she said.

It was then that Abby Hayes had her brainstorm. It descended like a sudden snow squall. New thoughts swirled furiously in her mind.

Her hand shot into the air.

"Yes, Abby?" Ms. Bunder said.

"I'd like to do a Student Spotlight," Abby proposed. "Aren't students as important as teachers?"

"Great idea!" Mason gave a one-two-three burp in approval.

Zach shot a paper airplane onto Abby's desk.

The girls applauded.

Ms. Bunder clapped her hands for attention. "Excellent idea, Abby. But can you do the Student Spotlight _and_ Gabby Abby?" she asked. "We don't want you to give up your advice column!"

Abby Hayes agreed to do two columns for <u>The Lancaster Lark</u>. (After all, writing is her favorite subject! It'd be like having two helpings of dessert after dinner.)

"Who will you profile?" Ms. Kantor asked.

Brianna flipped her long hair over her shoulder. "I'm the obvious choice," she said.

"Yay, Brianna!" Bethany echoed loyally.

"Interview the Mason Man!" Mason yelled.

"Me! Write about me!" Other kids waved their hands to get Abby's attention. But Abby Hayes already knew who she was going to profile. She was going to do a Student Spotlight on Natalie. And she was not going to tell Natalie until it appeared in the paper.

At her desk, Abby took out a fresh sheet of paper. The article would tell everyone about Natalie, she decided. At the same time, it would show Natalie who she *really* was. Natalie wouldn't be able to ignore all of her finer qualities when they were written in *The Lancaster Lark* for the entire class to read.

Abby was going to write the best article she had ever written in her life.

Student Spotlight: Natalie
Natalie is a new student in our school.

She has many talents and abilities. For example, did you know that she reads a book every day

Abby stopped in midsentence. This just wasn't exciting enough. She stared at what she had written and then ripped up the paper.

Question: Who does chemistry experiments in her basement, reads mysteries, and can transform herself into any character?
Answer: Her first name begins with N and ends with E.

Weren't these the same words she had used on Natalie over the last few days? If they hadn't convinced her yet, would they convince her now? The question and answer was a good idea, though. Abby folded up her second attempt and put it in her binder.

Natalie is a very quiet person with many talents. She never brags or says much about herself. If you get to know her, she *will always surprise you. She's also good at everything she does, except sports, which she doesn't like.*

This was much better, but Abby still wasn't satisfied. There was something missing. She didn't know what it was. How was she going to find it? Natalie *mustn't* shrug off her words again.

She tried to remember how she came up with the brainstorm for her family. She hadn't been thinking about it at all. It had just flown out of her mouth.

Was that the problem? Was she trying too hard? Maybe she had to take a break.

With a frown, Abby turned to Jessica. "What would *you* say about Natalie for a Student Spotlight? And don't tell her," she hurriedly added. "I want her to be surprised."

Jessica thought for a moment. "I'm really glad she moved into our neighborhood. I like the way she's always imagining things."

Abby scribbled down her words. "Great!" she said. "Thanks for the second opinion. I'll quote you in the article."

"Quote?" Brianna asked. "Does someone want a quote?"

"Sshhhhh!" Abby warned. She scanned the classroom quickly. Natalie was at the front of the room, adjusting her camera lens.

"I was just asking Jessica what she would say about Natalie for the Student Spotlight," Abby said in a hushed voice.

"You should have picked me to spotlight," Brianna said. "I *am* too busy, though. Natalie is a good second choice."

"Yay, Brianna!" Bethany cheered. She added, "I have lots of good things to say about Natalie."

"You do?" Abby said. She grabbed another piece of paper. "Tell me."

"What's all the excitement about?" Mason interrupted.

"Sshhhh!" Jessica said. "Abby's asking for comments about Natalie for the Student Spotlight. It's going to be a surprise."

Mason burped. "I can tell you lots about Natalie."

"This is great!" Abby cried. Suddenly, she knew exactly what she had to do. She would interview the entire class. She would add everyone's ideas to her own. She would come up with an article that even Natalie couldn't ignore!

Chapter 15

Thursday | Two weeks later

"There is safety in numbers."

The Alphabet Calendar

Number of kids in Ms. Kantor's class who contributed to the Student Spotlight: 25

Number of teachers who contributed: 5

Number of compliments Natalie got: 72

Number of suspicious looks Natalie gave me: 0 (ha-ha-ha-ha-<u>ha</u>!)

Today the third issue of <u>The Lancaster Lark</u> will be published. What will Natalie say? I am more nervous about this column than about Gabby Abby. Thank goodness there is safety in numbers! If the entire class and all the teachers (even Mr. Raphael!) appreciate Natalie, she won't be able to say, "Abby, stop it." If thirty-one people have something positive to say about her, she will <u>have</u> to listen. Won't she?

Stay tuned! Don't touch that dial! Your fifth-grade Advice Columnist, Student Spotlighter, and Secret Star Reporter will report all new developments as they occur!

10:07 a.m. We are printing out the first copies of <u>The Lancaster Lark</u>. Jessica whispers to me that the Student Spotlight is on the first page, next to "Conversations with Brianna"!

10:12 a.m. Jessica hands me one of the first copies of the paper. The Student Spotlight looks even more official in print. I read over everyone's comments about Natalie.

Mason said, "Her ideas are as good as the boys'! Sometimes they're better."

Bethany said, "I loved when she took pictures of me and Blondie. She really understands how to get the best from a hamster."

Brianna said, "She's almost as good an actress as me."

Zach said, "I like her sense of humor."

Ms. Bunder said, "Natalie is a student with a very fertile imagination."

Mr. Raphael said, "I look forward to her continued progress in art class."

<u>Everyone</u> has something good to say about Natalie.

10:17 a.m. Natalie is taking pictures of the class reading <u>The Lancaster Lark</u>. She still hasn't looked it over herself.

10:29 a.m. Ms. Bunder hands Natalie a copy of the newspaper. "I think you'll enjoy this, Natalie," she says. She smiles in my direction.

10:30 a.m. I have butterflies in my stomach.

(Question: Why butterflies? Why not grasshoppers? Or cicadas? Or dragonflies?)

Okay, I have a whole colony of insects

flying, buzzing, and jumping inside my stomach! I wish they would settle down.

10:31 a.m. Natalie turns red. She shakes her head. For a moment, she looks at me, then she looks back down at the newspaper again.

10:32 a.m. She is still reading. Her face is still red. She keeps shaking her head.

10:36 a.m. She finishes the article. She stares straight ahead. Her eyes are glassy. She appears dazed.

Bethany comes over and hugs her. "It's all true!" she says to Natalie. "Every word of it!"

(Reminder to self: Never complain about Bethany's rodent stories again! Pretend fascination with hamster adventures! Smile when Bethany says, "Yay, Brianna!" for the quadrillionth time.)

10:41 a.m. Lots of kids are congratulating Natalie. She is smiling now. Her eyes are sparkling. She is sitting up straight in her chair. I wave to her. She waves back and mouths the words "thank you!"

10:58 a.m. Natalie frees herself from the crush of kids surrounding her. She comes over to me. "I never knew so many people liked me," she says in astonishment. "They really do, don't they? Even Mr. Raphael."

I nod in agreement.

She hugs the article against her chest. "I'll never forget this, Abby. This is the nicest thing anyone has ever done for me in my life."

Hooray! Hooray! Hooray! It <u>worked</u>! Do jig in middle of fifth-grade classroom! Skip downstairs to cafeteria! Hop on one foot all the way to recess!

The pen <u>is</u> mightier than the sword!

What should Gabby Abby do next? Tackle the issue of world peace? Ease pains of suffering humanity? Solve one problem free for every two sent to the advice column? (That won't work. They're <u>all</u> free!)

Anything is possible.

Oops, another letter from Sore Ears in my

mailbox. His parents got annoyed at him for smiling when they yelled! He wants more advice!

Yikes! What do I say now?

Maybe I'll tell him not to take Gabby Abby's advice so seriously. I'm only ten years old. I'm not supposed to know <u>everything</u>.

But I do know <u>some</u> things.

Like figuring out that Heather can stay at our house while my parents help Great-uncle Jack. And how to let Natalie know that her friends care about her.

Hooray! Hooray! The world is my oyster! (Why not lobster? Or crawfish? Or shrimp? Or – oh, never mind!)